W9-CDN-627

AT THE CRACK OF THE BAT

Other Books by Lillian Morrison

Poetry

The Ghosts of Jersey City
Miranda's Music (with Jean Boudin)
The Sidewalk Racer
Who Would Marry a Mineral?
Overheard in a Bubble Chamber
The Break Dance Kids

Poetry Anthologies

Sprints and Distances
Rhythm Road

Folk Rhyme Collections

Yours Till Niagara Falls
Black Within and Red Without
A Diller, A Dollar
Remember Me When This You See
Touch Blue
Best Wishes, Amen

Baseball Poems Compiled by

Lillian Morrison

Illustrated by Steve Cieslawski

Hyperion Books for Children · New York

Printed in the United States of America.
For information address Hyperion Books for Children,
114 Fifth Avenue, New York, New York 10011.

First Edition
1 3 5 7 9 10 8 6 4 2
Library of Congress Cataloging-in-Publication Data
At the crack of the bat/compiled by Lillian Morrison:
illustrated by Steve Cieslawski—1st ed.
p. cm.
Summary: An illustrated collection of poems, by a variety of
authors, about the game and personalities of baseball.
ISBN 1-56282-176-8 (trade)—ISBN 1-56282-177-6 (lib. bdg.)
1. Baseball—Juvenile poetry. 2. Children's poetry, American.
[1. Baseball—Poetry. 2. American poetry—Collections.]
I. Morrison, Lillian. II. Cieslawski, Steve, ill.
PS95.B33A86 1992 811.008'0355—dc20 91-28946 CIP AC

Acknowledgments

For permission to use certain poems in this anthology, grateful acknowledgment is made to the following:

Richard Armour. "Numbers Game" from *All in Sport.* Copyright © 1972 by Richard Armour. Reprinted by permission of McGraw-Hill, Inc. **Scott Barry.** "Hail" from *Pulsar.* Copyright © 1972 by the Buffalo and Erie County Public Library. Reprinted by permission of the author. **Milton Bracker.** "The Home-Watcher," "Tomorrow!" and "Wamby, or the Nostalgic Record-Book," copyright © 1962 by The New York Times Company. Reprinted by permission. **Tom Clark.** "The Great One" from *Fan Poems.* Copyright © 1976 by Tom Clark. **Lucille Clifton.** "Jackie Robinson" from *An Ordinary Woman.* Copyright © 1974 by Lucille Clifton. Reprinted by permission of Curtis Brown, Ltd. **Hester Jewell Dawson.** "October" from *Stone Country,* Fall / Winter 1986 / 87. Reprinted by permission of the author. **Stephen Dunn.** "Outfielder" from *Bits, 9.* Copyright © 1979 by Bits Press. Reprinted by permission of the author. **R. Gerry Fabian.** "Bottom of the Ninth Haiku" and "Pull Hitter" from *Double Header,* published by Samisdat. Copyright © 1983 for R. Gerry Fabian. Reprinted by permission of the author. **B. H. Fairchild.** "For Junior Gilliam (1928–1978)" from *The Little Magazine,* vol. 13, no. 3 & 4. Reprinted by permission of the author. **Gene Fehler.** "Nolan Ryan" and "Winner" from *Center Field Grasses: Poems from Baseball.* Copyright © 1991 by Gene Fehler. With permission of McFarland & Company, Inc., Publishers, Jefferson, NC. **Robert Francis.** "The Base Stealer." Reprinted from *The Orb Weaver.* Wesleyan University Press. Copyright © 1948 by Robert Francis. By permission of University Press of New England. **Ford Frick.** "Along Came Ruth" from *Games, Asterisks and People: Memoirs of a Lucky Fan* by Ford C. Frick. Copyright © 1973 by Ford C. Frick. Reprinted by permission of Crown Publishers, Inc. **Robert L. Harrison.** "The Baseball Card Dealer" from *Spitball,* Summer 1986 (under the title "Dealer's Lament"). Reprinted by permission of the author. **Conrad Hilberry.** "Instruction" from *Bits 3.* Copyright © 1976 by Robert Wallace. Reprinted by permission of the author. **Jonathan Holden.** "How to Play Night Baseball" from *Design for a House: Poems* by Jonathan Holden by permission of the University of Missouri Press. Copyright © 1972 by the author. **X. J. Kennedy.** "The Abominable Baseball Bat." from *The Phantom Ice Cream Man.* Copyright © 1975, 1977, 1978, 1979 by X. J. Kennedy. Reprinted by permission of Curtis Brown, Ltd. **Robert Lord Keyes.** "The Yankees" from *Spitball,* Fall 1986. Reprinted by permission of the author. **Jim LaVilla-Havelin.** "What the Diamond Does Is Hold It All In" from *What the Diamond Does Is Hold It All In.* White Pine Press, Buffalo, NY. Copyright © 1978 by Jim LaVilla-Havelin. **Mark Lukeman.** "Playing Stickball with Robbie Shea" from *Spitball,* Winter 1988. Reprinted by permission of the author. **Mike Makley.** "The New Kid." Copyright © 1975. Reprinted by permission of the author. **D. Roger Martin.** "Hammerin' Hank" from *70 on the 70's.* Published by the Ashland Poetry Press and reprinted with their permission. **Eve Merriam.** "End of Winter" from *A Sky Full of Poems* by Eve Merriam. Copyright © 1964, 1970, 1973 by Eve Merriam. Reprinted by permission of Marian Reiner for the author. **Marianne Moore.** "Baseball and Writing," copyright © 1961 Marianne Moore, © renewed 1989 by Lawrence E. Brinn and Louise Crane, Executors of the Estate of Marianne Moore. From *The Complete Poems of Marianne Moore* by Marianne Moore. Used by permission of Viking Penguin, a division of Penguin Books USA Inc. **Lillian Morrison.** "Donnybrook at Riverfront Stadium," copyright © 1992 by Lillian Morrison. Used by permission of the author. **Raymond Souster.** "The Ballad of Old Rocky Nelson" is reprinted from *Collected Poems of Raymond Souster* by permission of Oberon Press. **Chuck Sullivan.** "Stickball." First published in *Esquire* October 1974. Reprinted courtesy of the Hearst Corporation. **Jacqueline Sweeney.** "First Time at Third," copyright © 1992 by Jacqueline Sweeney. Used by permission of Marian Reiner for the author. **May Swenson.** "Analysis of Baseball," copyright © 1971 by May Swenson and used with the permission of the Literary Estate of May Swenson. **Steve Vittori.** "Tinker to Evers?" appeared in *Spitball,* no. 31, Fall 1989, p. 35. Used by permission of Steve Vittori. **The New York Yankees** trademark as depicted on page 28 is reproduced with permission of Major League Baseball Properties, Inc.

Contents

Preface

Baseball is America's favorite sport, and some people are so taken with the game that they write poems about it. They write about the teams, the players, and the plays. They write about the exciting action in the big leagues and also about what it's like for the rest of us who play catch and take a turn at bat in backyards, neighborhood parks, and playgrounds.

Whether you play in Little League or in pickup games or are just a fan who saves baseball cards and likes to root for your special major league team, you will recognize some of the feelings expressed in these poems and some of the happenings described. You will also, I hope, experience again the fun, the suspense, the high moments (and sometimes low ones) of this terrific sport.

And as an extra added bonus, you may, if you are lucky, come to know the excitement and pleasure to be found in words and rhythms as well.

—*Lillian Morrison*

Take Me Out to the Ball Game

Take me out to the ball game,
Take me out with the crowd.
Buy me some peanuts and cracker jack;
I don't care if I never get back.

Let me root, root, root for the home team,
If they don't win it's a shame
For it's one, two, three strikes you're out
At the old ball game.

Jack Norworth

The Yankees

The Yankees are in spring training
down in Florida.
I can feel them every day
cracking their bats on anvils
with each warmer sunrise.
The Yankees pound quarters
out of the moon.
The Yankees
knock birds out of trees
by the millions.
I can listen to them
chewing up the college squads
and minor leaguers
like wolves on a deer.
It is a thing to hear.

The snow
listens so hard it vanishes.
The pastures
clear themselves of everything
but wind.

The ponds collapse,
the ground moves.

The Yankees
are heading north.

Robert Lord Keyes

Tomorrow!

Hoorah, hooray!
Be glad, be gay—
The best of reasons
Is Opening Day.

And *cheering the players*
And *counting the gate*
And *running the bases*
And *touching the plate.*

And *tossing the ball out*
And *yelling Play Ball!*
(Who cares about fall-out—
At least, until fall?)

Let nothing sour
This sweetest hour:
The baseball season's
Back in flower!

Milton Bracker

End of Winter

Bare-handed reach
to catch
April's
incoming curve.
   Leap
     higher than you thought you could
       and
Hold:
   Spring,
   Solid,
   Here.

Eve Merriam

Analysis of Baseball

It's about
the ball,
the bat,
and the mitt.
Ball hits
bat, or it
hits mitt.
Bat doesn't
hit ball, bat
meets it.
Ball bounces
off bat, flies
air, or thuds
ground (dud)
or it
fits mitt.

Bat waits
for ball
to mate.
Ball hates
to take bat's
bait. Ball
flirts, bat's
late, don't
keep the date.
Ball goes in
(thwack) to mitt,
and goes out
(thwack) back
to mitt.

Ball fits
mitt, but
not all
the time.
Sometimes
ball gets hit
(pow) when bat
meets it,
and sails
to a place
where mitt
has to quit
in disgrace.
That's about
the bases
loaded,
about 40,000
fans exploded.

It's about
the ball,
the bat,
the mitt,
the bases
and the fans.
It's done
on a diamond,
and for fun.
It's about
home, and it's
about run.

May Swenson

Pull Hitter

At
the
CRACK
of the bat
a l o n g drive
c
u
r
v
i
n
g
Foul!

R. Gerry Fabian

Hitting

When you're hot, you're hot.
When you're not, you're not.

The Abominable Baseball Bat

I swung and swung at empty air
And when I heard the umpire
Behind me shout, "Strike three—you're out!"
My bat turned to a vampire.

The whole team had to pry it loose.
Poor Ump looked sort of flat.
Now ever since, my bat and I
Walk every time we bat.

X. J. Kennedy

Numbers Game

One runner's safe, one runner's out,
Or so the ump has beckoned.
The one who's safe touched second first,
The one who's out, first second.

Richard Armour

Outfielder

So this is excellence: movement
toward the barely possible—
the puma's dream
of running down a hummingbird
on a grassy plain.

Stephen Dunn

How to Play Night Baseball

A pasture is best, freshly
mown so that by the time a grounder's
plowed through all that chewed, spit-out
grass to reach you, the ball
will be bruised with green kisses. Start
in the evening. Come
with a bad sunburn and smelling of chlorine,
water still crackling in your ears.
Play until the ball is khaki—
a movable piece of the twilight—
the girls' bare arms in the bleachers are pale,
and heat lightning jumps in the west. Play
until you can only see pop-ups,
and routine grounders get lost in
the sweet grass for extra bases.

Jonathan Holden

The Base Stealer

Poised between going on and back, pulled
Both ways taut like a tightrope-walker,
Fingertips pointing the opposites,
Now bouncing tiptoe like a dropped ball
Or a kid skipping rope, come on, come on,
Running a scattering of steps sidewise,
How he teeters, skitters, tingles, teases,
Taunts them, hovers like an ecstatic bird,
He's only flirting, crowd him, crowd him,
Delicate, delicate, delicate, delicate—now!

Robert Francis

Instruction

The coach has taught her how to swing,
run bases, slide, how to throw
to second, flip off her mask for fouls.

Now, on her own, she studies
how to knock the dirt out of her cleats,
hitch up her pants, miss her shoulder
with a stream of spit, bump
her fist into her catcher's mitt,
and stare incredulously at the ump.

Conrad Hilberry

Donnybrook at Riverfront Stadium

Oh, what a melee
Oh, what a brawl
Oh, what a slambang
Free-for-all.

Managers, umpires
And 48 players
Rolled on the ground
In knots and layers.

Knight pushed Davis?
Davis shoved Knight?
Boys will be boys.
A bench-clearing fight.

The two were ejected.
Soto, Mitchell, the same.
Pitchers played outfield.
Some baseball game.

Lillian Morrison

Casey at the Bat

The outlook wasn't brilliant for the Mudville nine that day;
The score stood four to two with but one inning more to play.
And then, when Cooney died at first, and Barrows did the same,
A sickly silence fell upon the patrons of the game.

A straggling few got up to go in deep despair. The rest
Clung to that hope which springs eternal in the human breast;
They thought, If only Casey could but get a whack at that
We'd put up even money now, with Casey at the bat.

But Flynn preceded Casey, as did also Jimmy Blake,
And the former was a lulu and the latter was a cake;
So upon that stricken multitude grim melancholy sat,
For there seemed but little chance of Casey's getting to the bat.

But Flynn let drive a single, to the wonderment of all,
And Blake, the much despisèd, tore the cover off the ball;
And when the dust had lifted, and men saw what had occurred,
There was Jimmy safe at second, and Flynn a-hugging third.

Then from five thousand throats and more there rose a lusty yell;
It rumbled through the valley, it rattled in the dell;
It knocked upon the mountain and recoiled upon the flat,
For Casey, mighty Casey, was advancing to the bat.

There was ease in Casey's manner as he stepped into his place;
There was pride in Casey's bearing and a smile on Casey's face.
And when, responding to the cheers, he lightly doffed his hat,
No stranger in the crowd could doubt 'twas Casey at the bat.

TEAM 1 2 3 4 5 6 7 8 9 10
CINTI
MUDVL
CASEY
9

Ten thousand eyes were on him as he rubbed his hands with dirt,
Five thousand tongues applauded when he wiped them on his shirt;
Then while the writhing pitcher ground the ball into his hip,
Defiance gleamed from Casey's eye, a sneer curled Casey's lip.

And now the leather-covered sphere came hurtling through the air,
And Casey stood a-watching it in haughty grandeur there.
Close by the sturdy batsman the ball unheeded sped;
"That ain't my style," said Casey. "Strike one," the umpire said.

From the benches, black with people, there went up a muffled roar,
Like the beating of the storm waves on a stern and distant shore.
"Kill him! Kill the umpire!" shouted someone on the stand;
And it's likely they'd have killed him had not Casey raised his hand.

With a smile of Christian charity great Casey's visage shone;
He stilled the rising tumult, he bade the game go on;
He signaled to the pitcher, and once more the spheroid flew;
But Casey still ignored it, and the umpire said, "Strike two."

"Fraud!" cried the maddened thousands, and echo answered "Fraud!"
But one scornful look from Casey and the audience was awed;
They saw his face grow stern and cold, they saw his muscles strain,
And they knew that Casey wouldn't let that ball go by again.

The sneer is gone from Casey's lip, his teeth are clenched in hate,
He pounds with cruel violence his bat upon the plate;
And now the pitcher holds the ball, and now he lets it go,
And now the air is shattered by the force of Casey's blow.

Oh, somewhere in this favored land the sun is shining bright,
The band is playing somewhere, and somewhere hearts are light;
And somewhere men are laughing, and somewhere children shout,
But there is no joy in Mudville—mighty Casey has struck out.

Ernest Lawrence Thayer

The Ballad of Old Rocky Nelson

When old Rocky Nelson shuffles up to the plate
The outfield shifts round and the fans all wait.

He takes up his stance which ignores every law,
Has a last slow suck of the quid in his jaw,

And waits while the pitcher makes up his mind
What new deception his arm can unwind.

Then the ball comes in and the sound of wood
That's heard by the ear does the loyal heart good,

And the ball rises up like a hunted thing
Pursued by an angry bumble-bee's sting,

And the outfielders run but it's no use at all—
Another one over the right field wall.

And as Rocky trots slowly around the bases
Happiness lights up twelve thousand faces.

Raymond Souster

First Time at Third

First time at third
nothing but nerves.
He fists-whomps his glove,
tucks in his shirt,
kicks up the dirt
for the twenty-fifth time.

Gets in position
pumped up to win,
ump sweeps the plate.
Will it ever begin?

A quick line-drive!
He leaps for the sky.
His body's an arrow,
glove aimed high.

What's this?
He stumbles,
he tumbles to earth.
His glove is still empty,
face red as his shirt.

The game hasn't started?
"Play ball!" can be heard
and he's tried to snag
a lowflying bird;
fastflying, linedriving
feathers and all.

How could he think
that a bird was a ball!

Jacqueline Sweeney

NY
2

The New Kid

Our baseball team never did very much,
we had me and PeeWee and Earl and Dutch.
And the Oak Street Tigers always got beat
until the new kid moved in on our street.

The kid moved in with a mitt and a bat
and an official New York Yankee hat.
The new kid plays shortstop or second base
and can outrun us all in any place.

The kid never muffs a grounder or fly
no matter how hard it's hit or how high.
And the new kid always acts quite polite,
never yelling or spitting or starting a fight.

We were playing the league champs just last week;
they were trying to break our winning streak.
In the last inning the score was one–one,
when the new kid swung and hit a home run.

A few of the kids and their parents say
they don't believe that the new kid should play.
But she's good as me, Dutch, PeeWee, or Earl,
so we don't care that the new kid's a girl.

Mike Makley

Playing Stickball with Robbie Shea

At the wall
we play suburban stickball,
bat with a pitchfork handle
my grandfather
cut from his garden.
We pitch
tennis balls
light
as crisp apples.
Strips of electrical
tape
mark the strike zone
against
red school brick.
Rob throws strikes.
I swing hard
and miss. Robbie is so much better than me.
But today
the sky is blue,
summer is in our bones,
and so many things don't count yet.

Mark Lukeman

Stickball

In the middle
of the concrete heat
boys manning our
sneakered positions tarred
in the block's summer field

We hustled our
fates into shape
on the city's sweating face
in the lean, bouncing grace
of our broomstick, rubber ball game
bound by the sewers and parked cars
of our Outlaw Little League

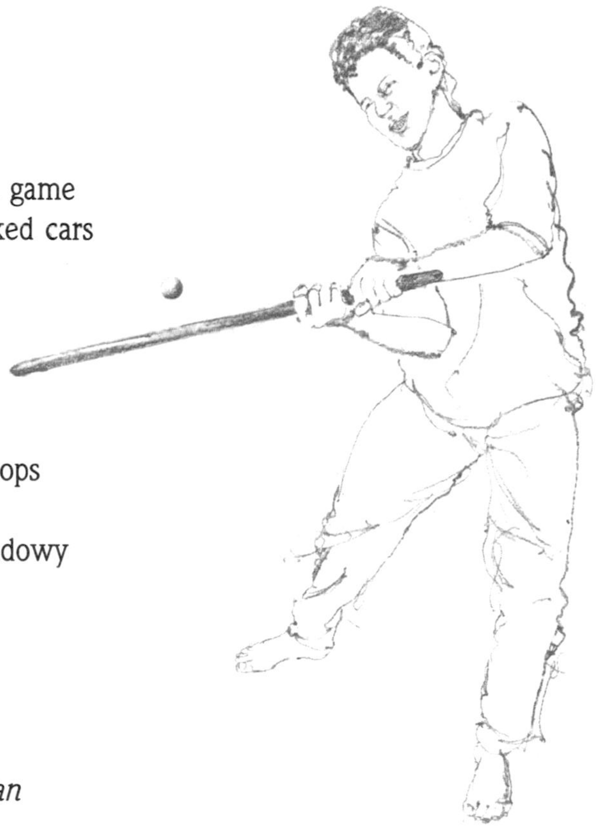

While on the sidelines
dreaming in cheers
the old men watched
bleachered on brownstone stoops
and iron fire escapes
making small book on the shadowy
skills of stickball stars
lost in the late-inning sun
of the stadiumed street's
priceless, makeshift diamond

Chuck Sullivan

Winner

what I remember most
is my dad behind the rusted screen
back of home plate
"You can hit this guy!"
his voice not letting up
through four fast balls
(two misses swinging late,
two fouls on checked swings)

then the curve ball and the dying quail
into left-center,
the winning run sliding home,
my dad all smiles,
slapping backs in the bleachers
as if HIS single had won the game

Gene Fehler

The Baseball Card Dealer

What price Goodens?
Mattingly make my day,
all the cards are mint I say.
Touch greatness,
feel heartbeats pressed
onto cardboard,
smell gum dust
and join the lines
waiting for a hobby high.
Give up your dollars
George Washington
never had a RBI.

Robert L. Harrison

He threw a white pea
fast faster faster fastest
of them all,
Try hitting a pea
with a toothpick
and you'll see what it's like
to bat against the
fast faster faster fastest
of them all.

Gene Fehler

José Canseco (jump rope rhyme)

Jose Canseco is a very nice man.
He hits all the home runs that he can.
How many homers did he hit today?
Let's count them up in a very new way.
One-a, two-a, three-a . . .

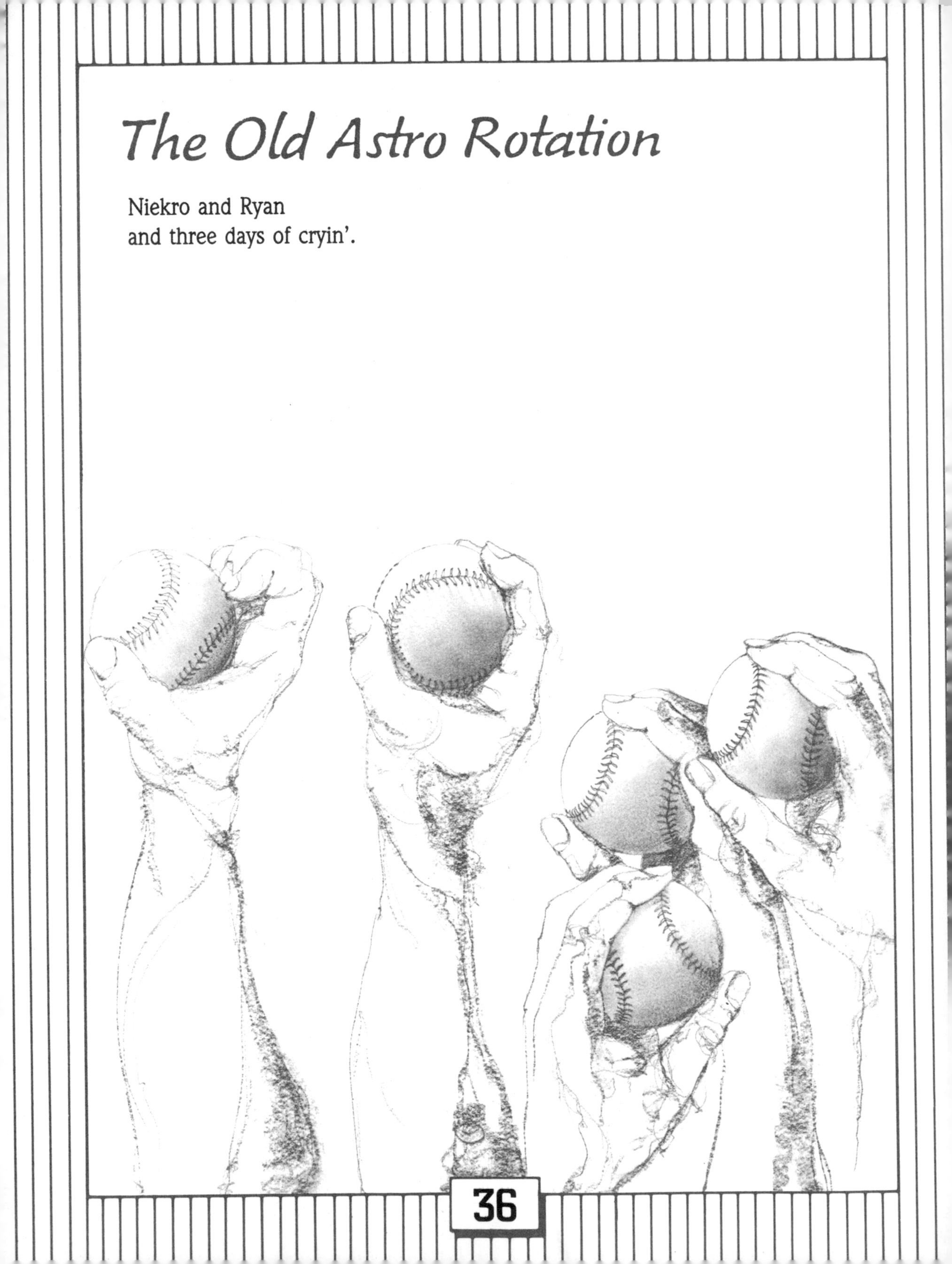

The Old Astro Rotation

Niekro and Ryan
and three days of cryin'.

Yankees, Yankees

Yankees, Yankees,
Boo, Boo, Boo.
Kick them in the ashcan
Two by two.

Red Sox, Red Sox,
Ray, Ray, Ray.
Put them on the field
And let them play.

375

Baseball's Sad Lexicon

These are the saddest of possible words:
    "Tinker to Evers to Chance."
Trio of bear cubs, and fleeter than birds,
    Tinker and Evers and Chance.
Ruthlessly pricking our gonfalon bubble,
Making a Giant hit into a double—
Words that are heavy with nothing but trouble:
    "Tinker to Evers to Chance."

Franklin P. Adams

Tinker to Evers?

For a ballclub to win in the National League
The infielders need to be versed
In the skills of sweeping the diamond
At shortstop and second and first.

Oh, where would Chicago's Bear Cubs have been
In nineteen hundred and eight
If the men who patrolled up the middle
Could only produce at the plate?

If with glove not of gold and hands lined with lead
Each knocked down balls with knees or with head;
Then reached down to launch a sub-orbital throw
To the home team dugout or seventeenth row?

Then Pirates and Giants would score on these terrors
Four runs on no hits but five or six errors,
On Merkle, on Tenney, on Bridwell; and Honus,
An infield double's your double-hop bonus.

And how would Franklin P. Adams describe
These choreographers' dance?
Why, just slap the ball up the middle.
Tinker to Evers? No Chance!

Steve Vittori

The Red Stockings*

We used no mattress on our hands,
No cage upon our face;
We stood right up and caught the ball
With courage and with grace.

George Ellard

*Baseball's first professional club, founded in Cincinnati in 1869.

Along Came Ruth

You step up to the platter
And you gaze with flaming hate
At the poor benighted pitcher
As you dig in at the plate.
You watch him cut his fast ball loose,
Then swing your trusty bat
And you park one in the bleachers—
Nothing's simpler than that!

*Ford Frick**

*He was commissioner of baseball from September 20, 1951 to November 6, 1965.

Jackie Robinson

ran against walls
without breaking;
in night games
was not foul
but, brave as a hit
over whitestone fences,
entered the conquering dark.

Lucille Clifton

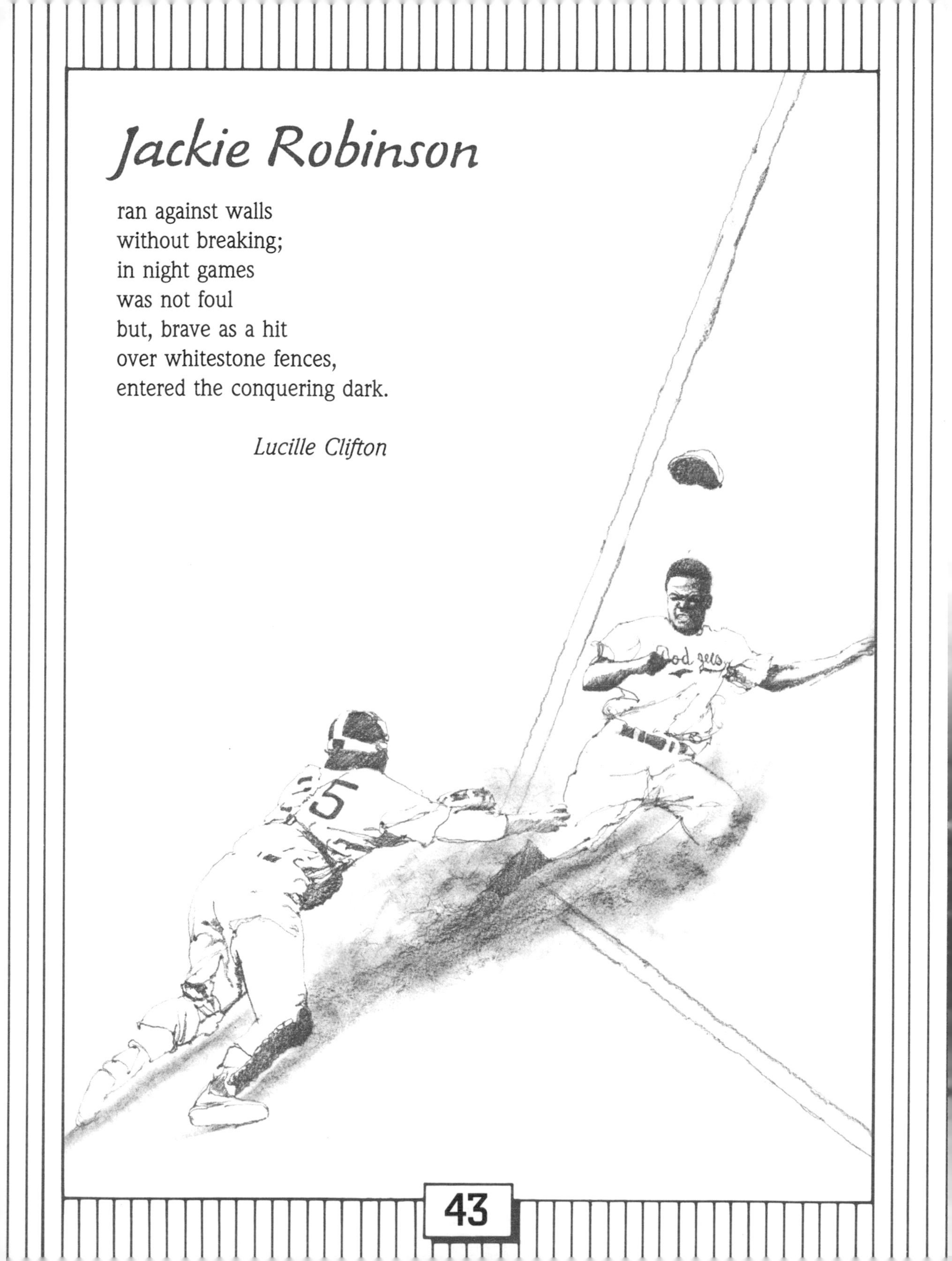

Hammerin' Hank

You did it, Henry.
You took The Babe's untouchable record
and stuffed it in your pocket.
Not bad for a gangling
black kid from Mobile.
The TV cameras were set to roll,
the reporters were poised
and the stage was set
with you and Al Downing
in the multi-million dollar spotlight.
Your teammate, Tom House,
caught the home run ball in the bullpen,
which was good economics.
That could have been
an expensive ball to buy back.
"A black Babe Ruth," they said you were.

Now it's your record
that stands casting its shadows—
a distant target
for future sharpshooters,
probably as yet, unborn.
And doesn't it make you wonder, Henry,
if things have really changed
since Jackie Robinson
courageously showed the world
there was another color of man
who could play this game.
Will any of us live long enough
to hear some wise scribe say,
"Here's a kid who
really has a chance to be
a white Henry Aaron."

D. Roger Martin

For Junior Gilliam (1928–1978)

Baseball and the waking
dream . . .
—Delmore Schwartz

In the bleak, bleacherless corner
of my rightfield American youth,
I killed time with bubble gum
and baseball cards and read the stats
and saw a sign: your birthday was mine.

And so I dreamed: to rise far
from Kansas skies and fenceless outfields
where flies vanished in the summer sun.
To wake up black in Brooklyn,
to be a Bum and have folks call me Junior
and almost errorless hit .280 every year
and on the field, like you, dance double plays,
make flawless moves, amaze the baseball masses.

You would turn, take the toss from Reese,
lean back and, leaping past the runner's cleats,
wing the ball along a line reeled out
from home and suddenly drawn taut
with a soft pop in Hodges' crablike glove.
And we went wild in Kansas living rooms.

The inning's over. You're in the shadows now.
But summers past you taught us how to play
the pivot (or how to dream of it).
And when one day they put me in at second,
I dropped four easy ones behind your ghost,
who plays a perfect game.

B. H. Fairchild

The Great One

So long Roberto Clemente
you have joined the immortals
who've been bodysnatched
by the Bermuda Triangle

When your plane went down
it forced tears out of grown men
all over the hemisphere
Al Oliver and
even Willie Stargell cried

You had a quiet
pissed-off pride
that made your countrymen
look up to you
even if you weren't
taller than they are

No matter how many times
Manny Sanguillen
dove for your body
the sun kept going down
on his inability to find it

I just hope those Martians realize
they are claiming the rights to
far and away the greatest rightfielder
of all time

Tom Clark

Wamby or The Nostalgic Record-Book

A player, name of Wambsganss,
Is known to lots of older fanss;
He thrilled even those whose tongues he twisted
By his triple-play-in-a-World-Series, unassisted.*

Milton Bracker

*It happened back in 1920 and hurt the Brooklyn Robins plenty.

Spahn and Sain

Spahn and Sain,
Pray for rain.

Mister October, Reggie Jackson

When the leaves began to brown
Reggie's bat would go to town.

Bottom of the Ninth Haiku

The bases loaded—
two outs and three runs behind;
no one to pinch-hit.

R. Gerry Fabian

And what if you tire
   Before the last inning,
With one team on fire
   But not sure of winning—
Or even get dozy
   Before the decision?
There's nothing so cozy
   As television.

Milton Bracker

hail

hail
the way I see it,
no matter
how
sleetior/heatior/meteorologists
try to explain it,
hail
is still
tail
ends of doubleplays
turned over by
trillions of
very tiny, very trained
very sideways, very cirrus,
secondbasemen people
throwing little
snowballs.
ah.

Scott Barry

Baseball and Writing

(Suggested by post-game broadcasts)

Fanaticism? No. Writing is exciting
and baseball is like writing.
  You can never tell with either
    how it will go
    or what you will do;
  generating excitement—
  a fever in the victim—
  pitcher, catcher, fielder, batter.
          Victim in what category?
*Owl*man watching from the press box?
          To whom does it apply?
          Who is excited? Might it be I?

Marianne Moore

From the autograph album

If at first you don't succeed,
Slide for second.

In curve, out curve,
Slow ball, drop.
Don't forget Jim
The star shortstop.

Life and baseball
Are just the same;
You must strike hard
To win the game.

What the Diamond Does Is Hold It All In

the game ends in the air
centerfielder,   dashing to the wall
timing his jump

we know we'll cheer and rise
when it ends
                    our cars' headlights
                    in the parkinglot
                    will criss-cross the night air
                    like fireflies

but why a homer?
                            the long fly ball with no outs
                            scores the man from third
                            just as jubilant
                            with the winning run—
                            an arc we watch with cheers
                                     rising
                                            in our throats

the game ends
                    and we cheer

we rise
          our cheers rise
                              into the air

someone has shredded their program and
confetti litters down upon us

summer snow
in the air
a crucial series
won

the slight wind flaps at the flag
again
and fireworks strike the air
like screams

timing his jump camping under it
the game
ends

Jim LaVilla-Havelin

408

October

the high fly ball,
arches out above left field,
hangs there in the sky
outblazing the sun
while fifty thousand heads swing and cry
"Over the wall! Over the wall!"

then hold, fixed and dumb
as the ball drops
down and down, a dead bird
into a waiting glove

and there you have it: the song,
the flight, the perilous whisper of truth
or of love or possibly of faith

then the descent
and the end of the game

Hester Jewell Dawson

Notes on Ballplayers

"Donnybrook at Riverfront Stadium"—The Cincinnati Reds were at bat against the New York Mets. Eric Davis, Reds outfielder and heavy hitter (he hit three grand slams in one month in 1987 and has twice hit three homers in one game) had a shoving match with Ray Knight, Mets third baseman. Mario Soto was the Reds pitcher. Kevin Mitchell, now a power hitter for the San Francisco Giants, was a Mets outfielder.

"The Baseball Card Dealer"—Dwight "Doc" Gooden, Mets pitcher, was National League Rookie of the Year in 1984 and won the Cy Young Award for his 1985 season with 24 wins, 4 losses. Don Mattingly, New York Yankees first baseman, won the American League batting title with a .343 average in 1984, his first full major league season, and in 1985 was the league's Most Valuable Player.

"Nolan Ryan"—Nolan Ryan, now pitching for the Texas Rangers, is 45 years old as of this writing and has thrown 7 no-hitters during his major league career. He is the only pitcher to have thrown more than 4 no-hitters.

"José Canseco"—José Canseco, the Oakland A's slugger, was the American League Most Valuable Player in 1988. He hit 42 homers that year and had a slugging percentage of .569.

"The Old Astro Rotation"—The rhyme refers to the 1980–84 years, when Joe Niekro and Nolan Ryan were both pitching for Houston. Both were noted for striking out batters.

"Baseball's Sad Lexicon"—Joe Tinker, shortstop; Johnny Evers, second base; and Frank Chance, first base, were an excellent double play combination for the Chicago Cubs in the early part of the 20th century. They were elected to the Hall of Fame in 1946.

"Tinker to Evers?"—Fred Merkle, Fred Tenney, Al Bridwell, and Honus Wagner were National League infielders at the beginning of the 20th century. Merkle is famous for his "bonehead" play in New York's Polo Grounds in 1908. His failure to touch second base in a crucial game eventually cost his team, the Giants, the pennant. Honus Wagner, a great all-around and much-beloved player, was a Pittsburgh Pirates shortstop who hit at least .300 for 17 years in a row. His lifetime batting average was .329. He was elected to the Hall of Fame in 1936.

"Along Came Ruth"—George Herman "Babe" Ruth, also known as the Sultan of Swat, started as a pitcher for the Boston Red Sox in 1914, but in 1920, after having been sold to the New York Yankees, he became a phenomenal slugging outfielder. In 1927 he hit 60 home runs, a record for most homers in a season, which he held until 1961, when Roger Maris hit 61 in a season that was 8 games longer. Ruth retired in 1935 and was elected to the Hall of Fame the very next year.

"Jackie Robinson"—When Jackie Robinson began playing for the Brooklyn Dodgers in 1947, he was the first black player in the major leagues. That year, he led the National League in stolen bases and was Rookie of the Year. In 1948 he led all second basemen with a .948 fielding percentage, and in 1949 he led the league in batting. He was elected to the Hall of Fame in 1962.

"Hammerin' Hank"—Henry "Hank" Aaron, an outfielder for Milwaukee and Atlanta, is most famous for his 755 career home runs, breaking Babe Ruth's record of 714. He retired in 1976 and was elected to the Hall of Fame in 1982. Al Downing was the Yankee pitcher off whom Aaron hit his 715th homer. Tom House, Atlanta Braves relief pitcher, caught that homer in the Braves bullpen.

"For Junior Gilliam (1928–1978)"—Junior Gilliam joined the Brooklyn Dodgers as a second baseman in 1953 and was Rookie of the Year. After the Dodgers moved to Los Angeles he played all positions except pitcher, catcher, and shortstop. Pee Wee Reese, his teammate, was a star shortstop and captain of the Dodgers in the 1940s and 1950s, during which time the team won seven pennants. Gil Hodges, the great slugging first baseman on that team, later managed the New York Mets for eight years.

"The Great One"—Roberto Clemente was an outfielder for the Pittsburgh Pirates from 1955 until his death in a plane crash in 1972. The plane was carrying supplies to Nicaraguan earthquake victims. He was the National League Most Valuable Player in 1966, had a .317 career batting average, hitting .341 in 1971, and, in 1973, was the first Latino ballplayer elected to the Hall of Fame. Al Oliver and Willie Stargell, Clemente's teammates and fellow outfielders, were both noted for their batting. Stargell was the Pirates captain. Manny Sanguillen was the Pirates catcher who, in a gesture of despair at Clemente's drowning, dived into the sea, hoping to find him.

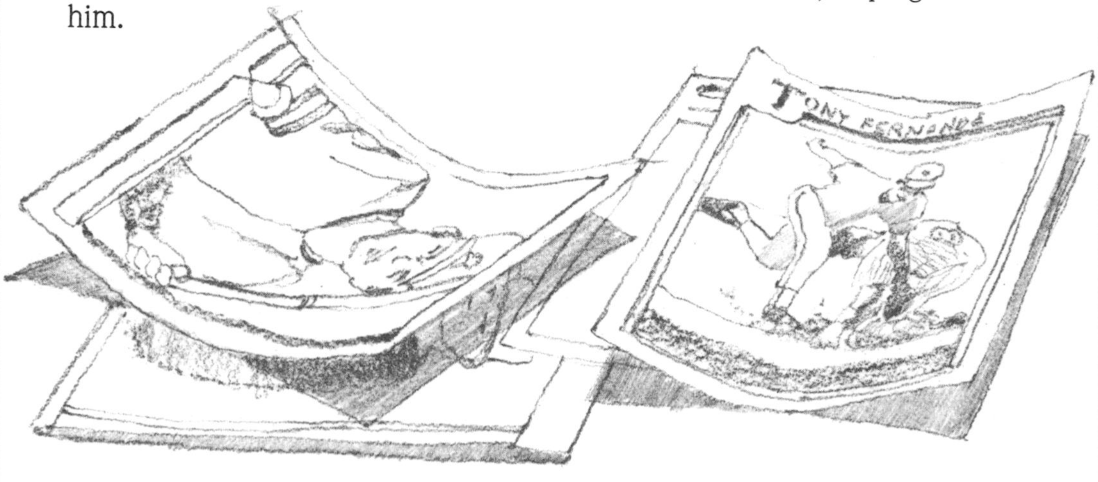

"Wamby"—Bill Wambsganss, an infielder for various teams in the American League and a good journeyman player, was a member of the Cleveland Indians when he made history with his unassisted triple play.

"Spahn and Sain"—Warren Spahn and Johnny Sain were outstanding pitchers for the Boston Braves. Spahn, a Cy Young Award winner in 1957, won 20 or more games 13 times and was elected to the Hall of Fame in 1973. Sain's best season was 1948, when he won 24 and lost 15.

"Mister October, Reggie Jackson"—Reggie Jackson, an exciting power hitter for various American League teams, is sixth on the all-time home run list with 563. As a Yankee in the 1977 World Series, he hit 5 home runs and had 25 total bases.

Author-Title Index